Clandestine
Angel

Angel Academy Book 2

KATE HALL

Lost Window LLC

"The treachery of demons is nothing compared to the betrayal of an angel."
Brenna Yovanoff

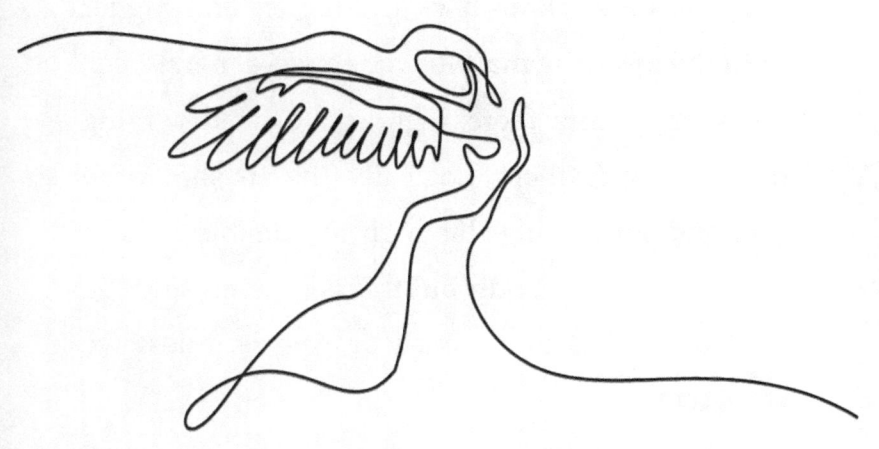

Chapter One

Flying is the best feeling in the universe.

I use my iridescent white wings to shoot myself up as high as I can, and then tumble back down, the clouds cool as the water vapor soaks into my wings, getting down beneath the feathers. My nearly white hair whips around me wildly, and I close my eyes. The rush of the free fall causes my heart to race. Just as I exit the clouds that constantly surround Theaa Academy, though, I unfold my wings, and they catch me like a parachute, glistening water droplets shaking from them with the sudden pressure.

I laugh and climb back up, higher and higher until the towering marble academy is a mere speck below me. From there, I glide, the wind ruffling me and my feathers. Logically, the air should be thin and suffocating this high up, unable to hold the weight of my body, but this is Heaven, and the laws of physics don't apply to Angels unless we want them to.

I allow myself to glide down in a lazy spiral, shifting my muscles and flight feathers subtly to get the best landing position. When I land, my bare toes embedding in the silky-soft and perfect-ly green grass, Nicolai, one of my closest friends, scowls at me.

I don't blame him. I got my wings mere weeks into our first term as students at Theaa Academy, a school that teaches angels to fight demons in the eternal war between Heaven and Hell. My expe-rience wasn't the norm, though. Nicolai has only had his wings for a week, having gotten them in the ritual that all students are supposed to partici-pate in at the end of their first term.

"It's hard to figure out," I insist, but my words

don't seem to make him feel any better. It had taken me months to be able to fly this well, and I'm still not nearly as good as Huỳnh or Gabe, the first friends I made here. Any reassurances they'd made hadn't made me feel better, either, so his unenthusiastic response isn't surprising.

He runs his hands through his snow-white hair in frustration. "I just don't understand how I can't do it. I got the top grade in our Intro to Flying class!"

I roll my eyes at him, but I'd been the same way when I was first learning to fly. It took me months of practice to get where I am now, and I'm still not as precise as the older students.. "You'll get it," I promise. I hold my hands out, and he takes them half-heartedly. I walk him through the first steps yet again, and he actually manages to get a few feet off the ground for just an instant. When his pace falters, I tighten my grip on his hands and lower him gently to the ground. "See? That's already better."

I take off back into the air. I shouldn't be showing off, but I can't help it. More than any other part of Heaven, flying is absolutely magical. It takes my breath away every time, and I feel like I'm on an impossible high whenever I take to the stars. Night is my favorite time to fly. As the sun sinks through the clouds on the horizon, I inspect the golden and pink light filtering through, bringing the castle to light almost like it's on fire.

"Hey!" Nicolai shouts from the ground, and then he flaps his brand-new wings. He gets the lift needed, but he doesn't have the balance to stay in the air for long, so he lands on his butt after a five-foot fall.

I laugh and swoop by him, and he grimaces.

And then, as happens every time I think too much about my happiness, the guilt creeps in. I'm not supposed to be here. Or, according to Death, I am supposed to be here, but only because I took someone's place.

And that someone is my girlfriend and true love, who is now trapped back at Daemaac Academy, a school for demons in Hell.

I grimace and dive back to the ground. Lately, I've been practicing a new move, which Huỳnh has been trying to teach me. I'm supposed to swoop down and then shoot back up a few feet, using my wings to hold me in the air as I float down gracefully. I don't land nearly that well this time, instead stumbling and planting my face in the dirt, but at least I don't tumble over the mountainside like I did earlier in the week. If anyone had seen that, I'd probably have gotten my Angel card revoked.

"That makes me feel better," Nicolai says with a giggle. He and I were on awkward terms for a little while last term, mainly because he kissed me and I was not even slightly into it, but we're back to our usual friendly banter at this point. The kiss has basically been forgotten.

"You know, you should be thanking me. Not everyone in our term gets a private tutor with the kind of experience I have." I raise an eyebrow, but, to nobody's surprise, he just laughs at my comment.

"Right. Experience," he says. Then, he swipes a finger over my nose. "And this is just an accessory?" He holds up the finger for me to inspect the clump of dirt sitting atop.

I roll my eyes and wipe my face with my hands, but they're dirty, too. I've probably just made it worse. Who knew that ethereal beings could get dirty?

"Incoming!" comes a shout from somewhere high above us. Nicolai and I step out of the way just as Huỳnh and Gabe simultaneously perfect the same maneuver I just completely screwed up.

"That's how you do it," Nicolai says, gesturing at them. "It's not even that hard!"

I glare at him, perfectly aware that the mud on my face will soften the look. "And would you like to demonstrate it for us? I'll give you a hint: you have to be at least fifty feet up to start it."

He sticks his tongue out at me, and I laugh at his scrunched-up face.

"What are we talking about?" Gabe asks, tossing an arm over each of us. He's in his fifth and final term at Theaa Academy. After this, he'll get to move to his permanent home in Heaven, and he'll only be called upon when he's needed. According to Azrael, it's at least a hundred or so years before most angels get called to action. There just isn't nearly as much demonic activity on Earth as there used to be, and, with the constant growth of Heaven, there are always more angels than are needed.

"How much Nicolai sucks at flying," I say. As Nicolai is about to protest, Huỳnh puts an arm around his other shoulder so we form a line.

"Awe, he's just a little tiny baby angel," she says in a cooing voice. His eyebrows scrunch together, and he frowns. We all laugh a little at his expense, and, after a moment of pouting, he joins our laughter. For someone who used to be a violent Russian gangster, Nicolai is always fairly good-humored. Heaven does that to people.

"Just wait," he says. "Once I figure out how to get in the air and stay there, it's over for you bitches."

I snort. "Sure. Let me know when that happens. Should I hold my breath?"

We walk back inside together. Tiffany, a term three student like Huỳnh, has a movie night planned for tonight, and we're all invited. Apparently, there's a huge entertainment center available at the dorms, similar to the magically-expanding bedrooms. Instead of containing beds and desks and closets, though, these rooms are made to entertain up to fifty students at once. Depending on what students want, there can be pools, tennis courts, and sometimes, like tonight, movie theaters with big fluffy floor pillows, always-full hot cocoa, and magically-appearing popcorn.

I get changed into a new set of pajamas—not the old ratty ones like my old pair from Earth, but a unicorn onesie.

I meet Huỳnh at the magical entertainment center door after we get changed into our pajamas.

I open my mouth to tell her about the note Desireé left me, the one I keep in the cubby I made for her, but I can't bring myself to get the words out. Maybe I'll tell her tomorrow. That's what I told myself yesterday, though. For now, though, I want to keep Desireé's promise all to myself.

Avery,

I will be long gone by the time you read this.

I love you.

I'm okay.

I will find you again.

Desireé.

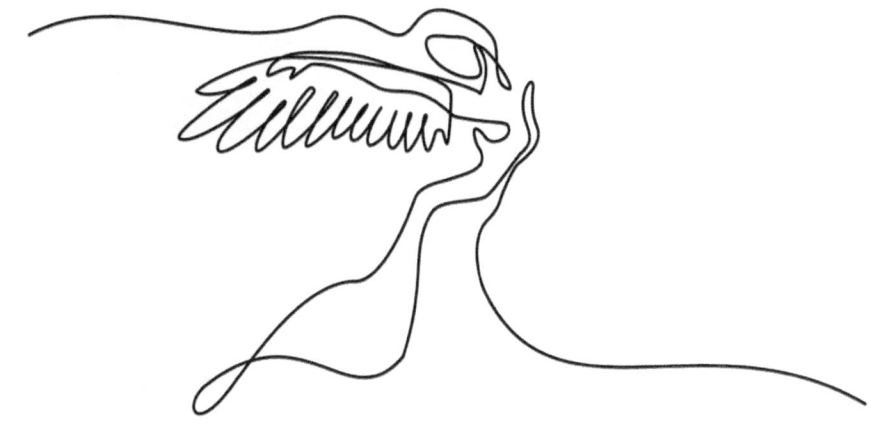

Chapter Two

When classes start up again for my second term, I'm curious yet unenthusiastic about the final class on the list. I space out during most of my other classes. I only have one martial arts course, and it's split by weapons now that we're past our initiation. I have a sword, so I'm in a class of mixed terms with other students that carry bladed weapons. Nicolai received a staff as his weapon at the end of last term, so he's in a different class than me. At least Huỳnh is here, and we chat before Gabriel, the famous Archangel and my fencing teacher from last term, comes in from his previous course. I avoid his eye contact, lest he figure out how uneasy he makes me. If any of the Archangels discover that I freed a demon instead of killing her, there will be serious consequences. I don't want to discover what those consequences are.

By the time I'm ready for my final class of the day, just after Advanced Enochian, my hands are practically shaking and sweating.

Demon Tracking and Awareness. I've had enough experience with demons to last an eternity.

Gabriel is standing at the front of the classroom when we walk in.

"Take your seats quickly," he says as we filter in. As he did in Fencing last term, Nicolai takes his place right beside me. His presence is comforting, and I try to focus on anything besides Gabriel, who has never seemed to trust me since I was found in my dorm with Desireé last term. Instead of an open room with space to use our weapons, there are thick textbooks and rows of neat desks.

As soon as everyone has sat down, Gabriel begins to speak, not even giving us a chance to absorb the new environment.

"Welcome to Demon Tracking and Awareness," he says, crossing his muscled arms and leaning against his desk. His black hair flops over his dark olive-toned forehead, and his eyes trace over each student as he says this. His golden-white wings are spread out behind him, taking up most of the front of the classroom.

I smile to myself when I look around to avoid his eye contact. I'm the only student here who doesn't have to wear a leather harness to contain my wings, as I'd been forced to wear it when I killed a demon and my wings sprouted prematurely at the beginning of last term.

"This will be the first of many field classes you'll be taking throughout your time at Theaa Academy. That means that, aside from classwork and assignments, we will be going to Earth to study demonic signs and track down demons." His eyes darken, and he frowns. "These are not childish field trips, and you are to listen to everything I say. Just as we can track them, demons are able to track down angels. You all have weapons now, and you will learn to summon them in your weapons classes before we begin our field work. You will need them."

Earth? We're going back to Earth? Gabriel's little speech sends a murmur through the room.

I swallow and straighten, and I'm not the only one who fidgets at this news. Since our deaths, we've only been to Earth once, and it was to hide out in a musty warehouse and kill the demons for our initiation.

Except what Gabriel doesn't know is that I didn't kill my demon. Instead, I'd helped free her.

"Yes, Daniel?" he asks, looking at someone sitting behind me. I glance back, and Daniel, an indigenous American boy who I shared a few classes with last term, messes with his long braid, which is pale like the rest of the young angels' hair. His is a strawberry blonde, so I assume it used to be black like Huỳnh's. Mine used to be dark blonde, so it's almost all the way white now. I haven't asked Nicolai what his looked like, but based on the brighter sheen, it had probably been perfectly blonde.

"Are we going to be fighting demons?" Daniel asks nervously.

We all watch Gabriel expectantly. This is the question that's on all our minds. The hairs raise up on the back of my neck. How many people are looking at me, the only person here who's supposedly killed multiple demons? It's a lie, though.

He shakes his head. "Most likely not. I ask that you have access to your weapons as a precaution, but it's very unlikely you will actually encounter a demon in person this term. And even if you do, you are less likely to have to fight it. We almost always try to capture the demons we find for future initiations."

Goosebumps rise on my arms, and I grind my teeth. Desireé had been one of the demons used for the initiation ceremony. If I hadn't been there, someone else probably would have killed her. I briefly wonder about the hundred or so extra demons that had been in cages, though. There had been far too many for our initiation alone. Why do the angels keep so many locked up when there are clearly more than we need? I frown at the insinuation.

When we're finally let go for the day, I leap out a

window, taking to the skies. Up here, I can breathe, and I don't feel like I'm being watched. All flying students are allowed to visit extra corridors of Heaven, but I haven't visited the city from our first visit outside the academy since our after-exam trip last week. I can't stand to see all those happy people, living in a blissful eternity that Desireé and I will never have together. If I go there alone, I just might break down.

Instead, I fly up and up and up, as far as my wings will carry me until I find one of the many floating mountains that dot Heaven. They're mostly unoccupied, and I lie at the top, spreading my wings and arms out behind me, relishing in the biting snowflakes against my hot, exhausted skin.

If I could stay up here forever, I would. This high, the stars are out even though the sun hasn't begun to set.

I unfold the note that I carried to class with me today. It had been a risky move, but I felt better having it on me. I reread the last line over and over again.

I will find you again.

The words are becoming smudged, mainly because I can't help but hold the note nearly constantly, opening and closing it several times a day and reading it obsessively.

I will find you again.

How will Desireé find me if she'd get killed at the slightest hint of her survival? Azrael told me that angels and demons who are killed go to purgatory, but I haven't actually found any information about what it's like there. Whatever it is, it must be worse than Hell. If it wasn't, demons wouldn't work so hard to avoid going there.

I frown, and then let out a frustrated groan. What am I supposed to do?

How am I supposed to make everything okay? If I can't be happy in Heaven, then there's absolutely no hope for me.

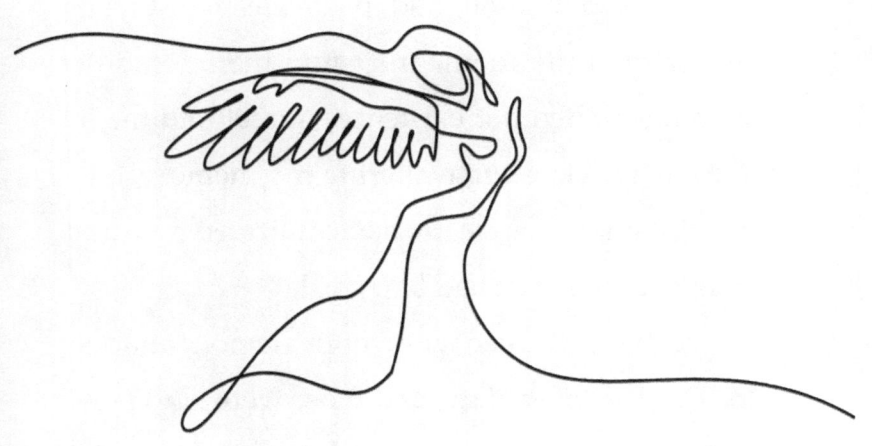

Chapter Three

My first term at Theaa Academy, there had been two demon attacks on the school. I'd only seen one demon each time, but there had been more that the Archangels and upperclassmen were fighting. As an upperclassman, Gabe had been involved, but he's never said anything about it, not even when Huỳnh or I badger him about it.

I'd killed the first demon when it attacked me, a feat that had shocked everyone, even the archangel Azrael. I hadn't even known that was something I was capable of doing. That was how I got my wings.

The second demon had been Desireé. She'd showed up at my room, and, until then, I hadn't even remembered her existence. Azrael told me it had been a trick, a curse altering my memory, but Cain, also known as Death, had confirmed my suspicions that our love had been real.

There haven't been any more demon attacks since Desireé showed up, and those were both fairly early in my first term. The other students seem to think that the breach had been discovered, but I know the truth. I see it in Azrael's eyes every time she looks out the windows.

The Archangels have no idea how the demons got in, and it's only a matter of time before it happens again.

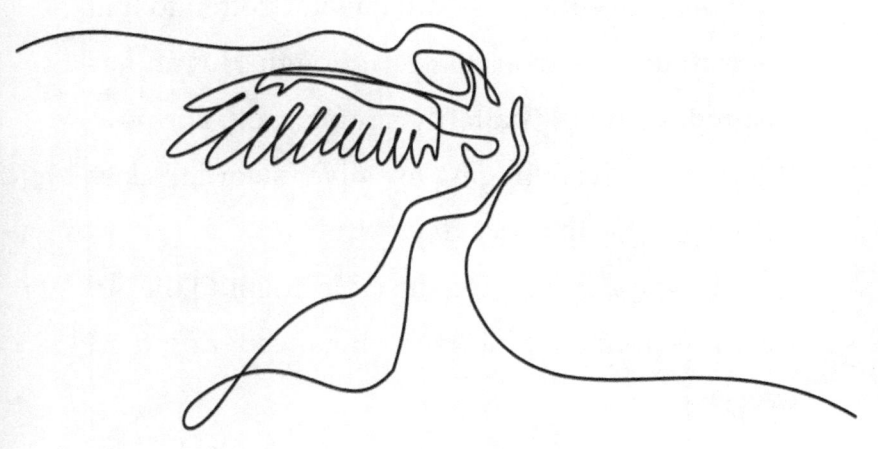

Chapter Four

It's the middle of dinner when a boom shakes the school.

We all pause, and I look up to Azrael, our headmaster who has taken me under her wing. Figuratively rather than literally. I thought she would look confident, but she looks…scared. It's a moment before she reacts, her eyes filled with fear for just an instant, although the other teachers have already sprung into action.

"Fourth and Fifth terms, at your posts," Gabriel calls, stretching his hand out and summoning his double-ended scythe. When will I learn to do something like that? We still haven't gotten to that point in our weapons class, although Huỳnh has assured me that it's a fairly simple spell. For now, though, I've been lugging my silver sword to class in its opal sheath every day.

Gabe leaps away from the table and into the air, the draft from his powerful wings scattering food everywhere.

He glances at Huỳnh and frowns, hesitating for just an instant before following Gabriel and the other Archangels out the window.

"It's going to be alright," I assure Huỳnh and Nicolai, who are staring out the window in shock. I've been involved in two of these attacks so far, and nobody has gotten hurt either time. Well, nobody other than me, but I wasn't supposed to be there. And, despite all the odds, I'd survived the first one. "They'll keep the demons away from the mess hall."

Conveniently, though, my sword is strapped at my waist from class earlier. I draw the weapon out and go to the window. I know I'm in no way qualified to defend anyone, as I'm just a second-year with a term of fencing and a week of actual sword training, but I feel the need to do something. I can't just sit around while the others are out there fighting demons. I may be in love with one, but I'd been brutalized and nearly killed by another. I'm not taking the chance that one gets in and kills Huỳnh or Nicolai—or anyone else, for that matter.

A girl in the term below me—it's easy to tell because she doesn't have wings—begins to cry, and her friends hold her and pat her back in reassurance.

"I thought it was supposed to be safe," she sobs.

I frown, the gears in my brain turning as I look around the mess hall.

"Everyone get into the back corner," I call over the rising panic of the room. The other students hesitate, and some raise their eyebrows, but I shout, "now!" and they go. A few third-years join me at the windows, weapons drawn and faces uneasy. Huỳnh has her twin daggers, which she clutches desperately. She looks at me, then sets her jaw. Her eyes harden, and she nods once.

"Hayes, Lashawna, I need you two in the rafters," she commands, and the two who'd come up with us look at each other then back at her before taking her order. They pump their wings, shooting up to perch on the arched beams that span the whole ceiling of the mess hall, Hayes's war hammer and Lashawna's flail at the ready.

I take a deep breath, then push it out forcefully.

We stand, tense in our positions, for what feels like hours, but could merely be minutes. My ears strain to listen to the clashing of weapons and the screeches of felled demons. I should be worried about getting killed, but I can't help but wonder if one of those screams belongs to Desireé. Eventually, though, even those sounds fade.

Enough time passes for the sky to go from pale blue to gold to black by the time a figure appears at the window. I tense, but my mind absorbs the white wings after a moment. Friend, not foe. I sigh and put away my weapon as Azrael enters. She looks exhausted, which rattles me. Azrael has looked concerned, frightened, and distant in the past, but I've never seen her tired. This is new territory for me. Can angels even get tired? I know I never have, other than the time I was knocked out by Azrael's spell.

She climbs in through the window, startled to find Huỳnh and I at attention, although we've put away our weapons by now.

Then, a small but proud smile comes across her face. She puts a hand on my shoulder. "Thank you," she says. Hayes and Lashawna float back to the floor, their weapons already gone as well.

She shakes the other guards' hands, and Huỳnh beams at her.

"Everyone should go back to the dorms," Azrael calls. "The threat has been taken care of. There's nothing more to be worried about."

I don't ask what she means by that, but the drawn look on her face makes me think that, whatever they've done, it isn't a permanent fix. There may not be demons in the school at this very moment, but there will be again. Until they can figure out how to prevent these attacks, they'll just keep coming.

Just like every other night since the initiation, I don't go to my huge bed, which was made to fit me and my gigantic wings. I go to the back of my giant walk-in closet, then open the hidden panel that's practically invisible against the back wall. That's where the room magically placed the cubby for Desireé to hide in during the weeks she was in the academy in secret. I have to curl my wings up against my back tightly, but the space is a thousand times more comfortable than my own bed as her scent wafts over me. I lie on my side, then glance up at the ceiling to study the space where she wrote my name.

I gasp and sit up too fast, though, smacking my head on the ceiling. I suck in a breath and lie back down, staring at the brand-new inscription that hadn't been there this morning.

I'm okay. I'll see you soon.

Desireé.

Below the note is a series of symbols that are familiar yet strange. Demonic runes. Maybe I should've paid more attention in that class last term, because I can't actually decipher them.

The handwriting is unmistakable, though, and nobody else knows this little room is here. Not even Nicolai, who has known the truth about me and Desireé, about Cain switching us, knows this one secret of mine.

No, this has to have been her.

Did she somehow manage to orchestrate the attack?

Was it all so she could send me a message?

I should be upset. Angels could've gotten hurt today, but instead, I smile. Just a little. Just enough that I'll definitely feel bad about it when I think about my reaction to this whole ordeal later.

Until now, I couldn't be certain that Desireé survived her escape from the cage on Earth or her return to Daemaac Academy. I'd been fairly certain, because if I hadn't convinced myself, then I wouldn't have been able to handle the days, but I hadn't known for sure. Now, though, a tension I've been holding for nearly two weeks floats right out of me.

If her note is true, I'm going to see her again. I never thought we'd see each other after I helped her escape. I'd saved her with the knowledge that we'd be separated for the rest of eternity. The note she'd left me had given me a little bit of hope, but this new inscription solidifies it.

Desireé is alive.

And I'm going to see her again, no matter what it takes.

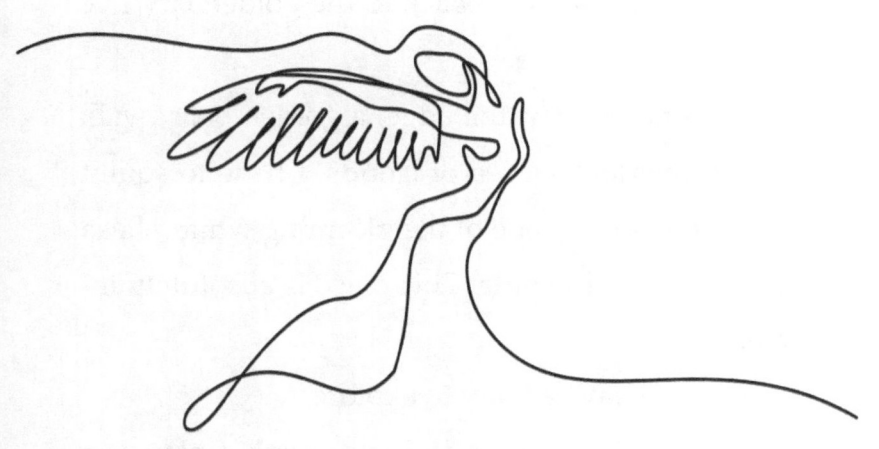

Chapter Five

The new note on the ceiling of the cubby keeps me going, my heart soaring every time I read it. It had been hastily scrawled, unlike the copies of my name that had been meticulously traced and burned in over and over and over again whilst she hid here. My fingers know the exact feeling of each letter within a few days of the demon attack, and I spend even more time out flying than usual. My energy is boundless, and this is the only way for me to find a release for all the feelings building up inside me.

Over the third weekend of the term, I even follow Huỳnh and Gabe back to the golden city I've been to once before.

We land right at the edge, a golden boardwalk which overlooks a sea of clouds. I have to squint to see the faint shape of the gleaming white Theaa Academy, and I smile. This place is absolutely incredible.

And we have all day to explore.

After the other two decide to catch a play at a palace-like theatre, I wander on my own. I'm far too restless to sit in a chair for a few hours, so I might as well attempt to enjoy myself. My eyes keep climbing up and up through the towering skyscrapers, and I have to ball my hands into fists in an attempt to quell my excitement. I shouldn't be having fun if Desireé can't be here.

Eventually, I wander into an electronics store. It looks almost exactly like one from Earth, except of course how clean and new everything looks from the glistening floors to the sparkling lights above.

It confuses me for a moment. I haven't seen anyone carrying electronics since I entered Heaven, although I can play movies that just show up on my white bedroom wall just by thinking about it. The concept of electronics mustn't be unfamiliar, but the actual existence of this store draws me in. What's the point of it, exactly?

Like most of the shops here, there are no employees. Why would there need to be when thinking about something can get you anything you want?

There are a few others browsing the aisles, and it's an odd sight to see angels with glowing white wings and hair in varying levels of paleness strolling through an otherwise normal electronics department store, their clothes ranging from elegant white renaissance robes to skin-tight yoga pants.

I pass a man with light brown hair, and I purse my lips when he can't see me. He must have been here quite a while to have hair that dark. Gabriel and Azrael both have plain brown hair, and they're some of the original Archangels, making them thousands upon thousands of years old. How old is this man, exactly?

I don't ask about it, though. It's probably considered rude. Still, I can't help but ponder. Will my hair ever become dark? I'd had dark blonde hair on Earth, so it seems unlikely, but still.

I eventually wander into an aisle that looks like it's carrying some sort of cell phones, except they're made of clear crystal in varying pastel colors. I experimentally tap across the screen of a pale pink device, but nothing happens. I must not understand them. Or maybe I can only use one when I graduate from Theaa?

I shrug and move on, exiting the store. There's no point wondering. I have eternity to figure it out.

Hopefully, it will be an eternity with Desireé. Except I have no idea how I could possibly pull that off.

I've only killed an hour by the time I'm standing out in the sun, so I find a cafe and get ice cream from the angel working at the front counter, a grin on her face.

"Enjoy!" she says, handing me the chocolate cone that's far more than I could logically eat.

I smile back. "Thanks!" Before I walk away, though, I pause. There are no customers behind me, so I ask, "Why do you work here? I mean, everything is automated, right?"

She glances at my clothes for an instant, then says, "Still a student? Yeah, most things are automated, but some of us like having jobs. Would you believe that some people even sit in offices all day working on spreadsheets?" She looks a little grossed out by the concept, but she shrugs. "To each their own. I guess some people really enjoy that sort of thing."

I laugh. "There's no way I could."

She smiles. "Me, either. But I do enjoy serving ice cream. It's all automated when I don't feel like doing it, and it's not like on Earth where customers would be mean. Everyone is so friendly up here. I mean, what is there to be angry about when you're in Heaven?" She laughs a musical laugh, and her own ice cream cone appears in her hand. She lifts it to me. "Cheers."

I smile and do the same, then find a seat to enjoy my ice cream. Somehow, I manage to eat the whole thing. It must be some sort of Heavenly magic that the absurd amount of rich chocolate doesn't make me horribly ill. Or that the dairy doesn't destroy my body.

I hadn't considered until now that I wouldn't be lactose intolerant here. I guess it makes sense, since eating isn't strictly necessary.

I spend the rest of the afternoon wandering around, and, just as I'm beginning to wonder what time Huỳnh and Gabe's play will be over, I see them turning the corner on the street ahead of me.

"Hey, guys!" I call, waving. I walk faster to catch up with them. "How was the show?"

Gabe shrugs. "Not terrible. I've seen better, though."

Huỳnh rolls her eyes. "Don't be a snob. It was good."

He smiles down at her, his eyes lingering long after she looks back at me. It feels like a private moment, so I turn my attention back to Huỳnh.

"What should we do now?"

The whole day, despite the pleasant company of my friends, I can't help but think about how much better all this would be if Desireé were here. Would she have stolen a bite of my ice cream? Would we have seen the play together, our fingers intertwined? I rub my thumb against my forefinger as though doing so means I can feel the letters from her note if I press hard enough.

I don't want to ruin Huỳnh and Gabe's day, though, so I don't bring it up. I keep catching their hands brushing together as we wander the streets, and I feel like a third wheel. A third wheel whose fourth wheel is missing.

And on fire.

And in Hell.

I frown, but they don't seem to notice my slowly souring mood. They're far too focused on each other, which I don't mind. I hate when people notice me too much. Although these two had helped me come up with a plan to free Desireé, I still don't feel comfortable talking to them about her. No matter what they did to help, they won't understand the relationship we have. And I will never forget the looks of confusion and near disgust they'd given me after I'd initially been found with her in my dorm.

"I think I'm gonna head back," I say when they make plans to watch the sunset from the top of one of the glass buildings. I might as well give them some privacy. There's clearly something going on between them, something new and exciting.

Something I can't have.

Yet.

"You sure?" Huỳnh asks, concern lining her face.

I nod. "Yeah. I was gonna help Nicolai with his flying again. He's getting better. If I work with him every day, he should be able to come out with us in a few weeks. He's learning a lot faster than I was since he's got the class every day."

Because I learned to fly from Azrael last term, I have a free hour while everyone else in my term is in flying classes. I usually use it to work on my assignments, not because I'm particularly inclined toward academics, but mostly because that gives me more time at night to lie in bed and think about Desireé.

When will I see her again?

The note says *soon*, but that's not exactly precise. A week? A month? A year?

A century?

It's all meaningless here, and I can't help but spend every moment of every day wondering if it will actually happen.

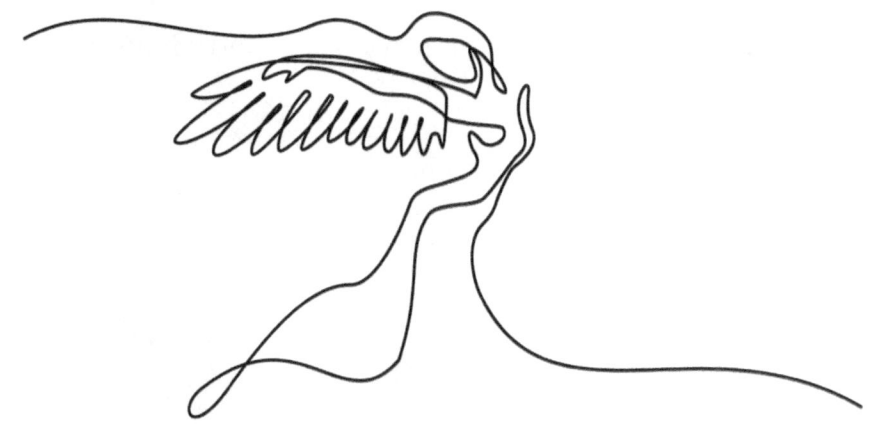

Chapter Six

It's only the third week of term when the school is attacked once again.

This time, though, they make it in through the mess hall windows before anybody notices.

There are guards posted at strategic points all around the mountain, so this shouldn't be able to happen. Demons shouldn't be able to sneak onto school grounds right under our noses. And yet, here they are. Their leathery wings and horns and clawed, ink-dipped hands are a dead giveaway, and the sulfur scent is just the cherry on top.

Huỳnh and I take up our positions at the windows just like before. Lashawna and Hayes dive down with their weapons at the ready, but there are just so many of them.

And what if Desireé is here again? What if someone kills her? Azrael and Gabriel dive out the window with a flock of fourth and fifth terms. If there are any in the room, there will be more dotting the mountain.

I'm so distracted by the imaginary image of Desireé being slain by Gabriel that I don't sense the demon before it grabs me from behind. I cry out as its claws dig into the muscles at the base of my wings, pinning me into the wall as my sword clatters to the ground.

"Don't say a word," it says, its voice hoarse. "I am only doing this as a favor."

It slams me against the wall again, and something heavy drops in the pocket of my blazer. I don't take too long to consider the implications, though, as the demon is ripped away from me, its claws tearing at my skin. Something hot and wet drips through my feathers. It must be my blood, and, when I glance at the ground, there are dots of liquid gold that have fallen down, staining the marble. It's beautiful and terrifying all at once. Angels aren't supposed to bleed. My head spins from hitting the wall so many times, but I have to focus.

I pick up my sword from the ground, the cool, leather-wrapped handle reassuring against my palm. Huỳnh has the demon in her grasp, and she's holding one of her daggers to its throat. The demon's skin hisses and bubbles where the blade touches it, and Huỳnh glances up at me.

I give the tiniest shake of my head, nearly imperceptible, and she relaxes her grasp just enough that only I notice. The demon slips away, kicking Huỳnh's feet out from under her, and dives back out the window. Behind Huỳnh, Hayes and Lashawna turn the last demon to dust.

The attack is over.

They got what they came for.

But what exactly was it? I don't reach into my pocket to find out, lest someone be watching. If it's discovered that we released the demon on purpose, there will be consequences.

There's something going on with the demons,

and I don't think I like it.
   Not one bit.

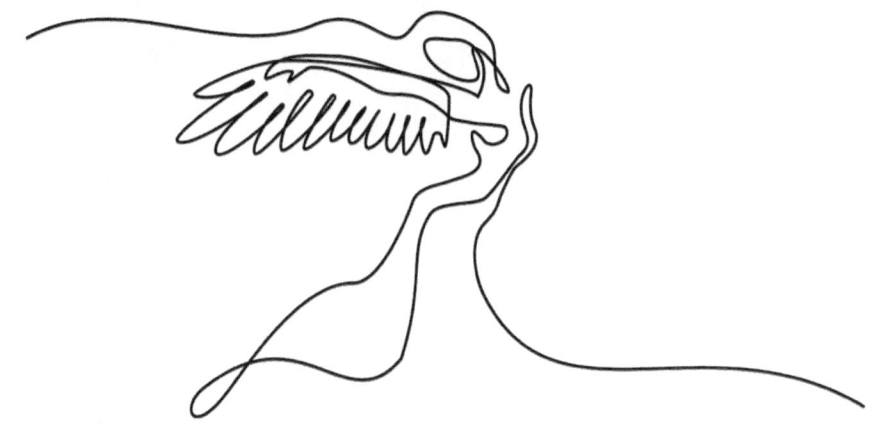

Chapter Seven

The object in my pocket is some sort of stone tablet. I lay in my hidden cubby, turning the thin slab over and over in my hands. It doesn't make sense. The surface is slick and pitch-black. Tourmaline crystal, or at least something similar. But why do I have it? Why did the demon give it to me? And why did that action seem to end the attack?

There are no new notes scratched into the ceiling, and I run my fingers over the last note once again. Had she been killed in the attack? Had she even come? Is this object a sign from Desireé? If so,

I'm not sure what it means. The demon had said that it was a favor, but I have no idea what the favor could have been.

I hold the small piece of stone in front of me, rubbing my thumb over it. It's no bigger than a cell phone.

My mind returns to the trip I'd taken to the city with Huỳnh and Gabe. I think of the clear crystal devices I'd found in the electronics store, but I hadn't been able to figure out how to use them. Is this one of those devices? Just a more…Hellish version?

I sigh with frustration and press the stone into the ceiling, right where Desireé had carved her note.

Immediately, the crystal goes hot, burning hot, and I gasp with pain. Yet, I can't get my fingers to release it. It's like I'm stuck here, my hand pressed into the stone which is, in turn, pressed into the ceiling. Tears prick at my eyes, and the pain radiates up my arm.

Just as quickly as it had arrived, though, the pain is gone. I release the device, and it falls and lands on my chest.

I stare at my hand, but it's not even pink. There is no burn, nothing to indicate that the device had harmed me in any way. What the hell?

Whispers float into my ears, hissing over each other in horrible, tempting patterns. I look around, but there's nobody here. Yet it feels like somebody is speaking directly into my ear in a language I can't understand.

Shakily, I pick up the tablet.

Dimly, as if through murky water, Desireé's demonic face stares back at me.

I gasp and drop the phone. Slowly, the whispers solidify and form real words, changing from several voices over top of each other into one voice that I know very well.

I grab the tablet and stare at it, squinting to make out her monstrous features that I know so well. "Desireé?" I ask, whispering as if someone else might hear me in my empty room.

A slow smile creeps across her face, and she looks wicked. With her fangs and blood-red lips and black eyes, though, she always looks wicked.

It's just a side-effect of being a demon.

"Avery," she says. The sound is quiet as a breath yet full, almost like she's in another room. There doesn't seem to be a volume control on this thing, and I have to strain my ears to hear her. "It worked!"

I smile, and the tears that had pricked my eyes from pain fall freely down my cheeks. She's here. Well, sort of. At the very least, I'm talking to her. I can see her face, no matter how dim it may be.

"Are you okay?" I demand. "What did they do to you?"

Her face darkens, and she avoids making eye contact with me. "I'm fine now." She doesn't answer the second part of the question, but I don't press. If she's uncomfortable talking about the awful things that happen in Hell, I won't force her to speak. "I don't have much time. And I wasn't even sure this worked. But I had to speak with you." Her eyes are alight with excitement the more she speaks. I can just barely make out her blue irises through all the darkness. "I love you, Avery."

I want to ask her so many questions, but she

looks away from me, her eyebrows contorting in fear. "I love you," I say with a rush, and she disappears.

I stare at the screen, but she doesn't return. I try pressing the device back against the demonic runes she'd carved in, but nothing happens this time.

I suck in a breath, and let it out with a long, slow shudder. Then, I close my eyes, running over the short conversation over and over again until I fall asleep.

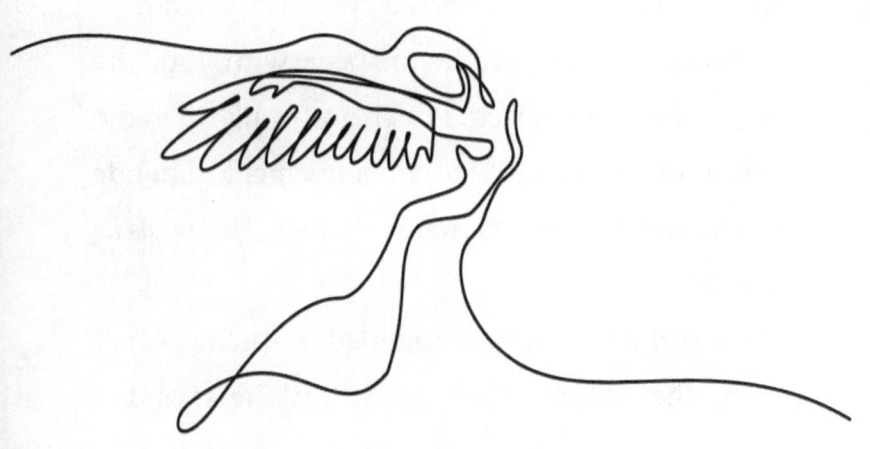

Chapter Eight

Gabriel does not look pleased with me when I walk into my weapons class the next morning, and my heart leaps into my throat. Did he find out about the phone? Does he know that Desireé has found a way to contact me all the way from Hell?

He doesn't look completely furious, though, so I try my best to keep eye contact with him. *Don't be suspicious. Don't be suspicious.* How am I supposed to make it through today knowing that someone could find out about my secret at any moment?

He ignores me for most of the class, but the class

draws to a close, he stares me down once again.

"Avery, Huỳnh, I'd like to speak with you," he says, an eyebrow raised. I flush and walk up to the front of the room, and Huỳnh joins me. My hands are shaking, so I clench them into fists. *He knows he knows he —*

"I heard about what happened in the mess hall during the demon attack yesterday," he says disdainfully. I open my mouth to explain, but he keeps going before I can speak. "I thought that both of you should know better than to take on a demon single-handedly, but you let it escape by not working together."

It's almost painful to force myself not to sigh with relief. He's mad that we didn't do a good enough job trying to kill the demon, not that we let it escape on purpose after it delivered a gift from my demonic girlfriend. I look to the ground in false shame.

"I'm sorry," Huỳnh says, taking a step forward. "I thought I could handle it myself when I got it off of Avery, but I was wrong. It got the best of me, and it escaped."

Gabriel nods, but his jaw is still tight. "Well, I'd like the two of you to come in after class for remedial training every day for the next two weeks. This type of mistake is unacceptable. What if, because of your mistake, that demon goes to Earth and harms some humans? Did you even think of the consequences of your actions?"

My heart races. "I'm sorry," I say as earnestly as I can muster, although I don't actually believe what I'm saying. It had helped me speak with Desireé. There was no way I could've let Huỳnh kill it.

"Me, too," Huỳnh says, her voice subdued.

After watching us for a long moment, Gabriel nods. "Take your places. Let's get started."

I sigh with relief and go back to my normal sparring area, and Huỳnh joins me. I can't believe we're going to have to spend extra time with Gabriel every day. What if he figures it out? An extra couple hours in the afternoons is a lot of one-on-one time with an ancient Archangel that's fought thousands of demons in his lifetime. Maybe even millions.

After classes end for the day, Huỳnh and I meet at Gabriel's usual classroom. He makes us run through drill after drill, and I'm mentally exhausted by the end of it. Trying to do each stance perfectly and memorize several new ones is tiring in itself, but I also had to keep from panicking too much about what would happen if Gabriel were to find out that Desireé is still alive. At least he didn't ask us any questions or try to make small-talk.

Huỳnh and I walk to dinner together, although we're silent through the meal while Nicolai and Gabe discuss the flying lesson that we'd missed from having detention.

Detention.

In Heaven.

I sigh. This place is not all it's cracked up to be.

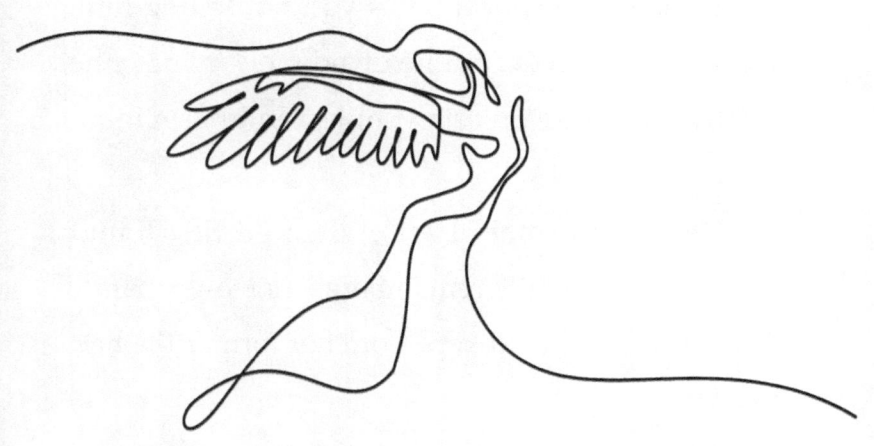

Chapter Nine

When I'm lying in bed later that night, my demonic crystal phone heats up once again. When it's done and the whispers slow, I stare at Desireé's face and smile, although she doesn't seem as overjoyed as I feel.

Probably from all the fire and brimstone and being surrounded by demons. I wish there were something I could do to make her feel any better.

We should talk about plans to get her out of there, or discuss how we're going to see each other again, but instead, she asks me to tell her about my day, and I tell her every little detail.

"Well, Marcus appreciates you not killing him. He's kind of a dick, but he owed me a favor." She finally cracks the tiniest of smiles, and I grin in return.

"He had a name?" I ask. When I'd first found Desireé, she hadn't remembered her own name. The only thing she'd kept from her former life had been me.

She nods. "Most do. That's what they hang on to. The smallest sliver of themselves." She pauses. "Before I found you," she says, her voice suddenly hushed, "they all called me Avery. Because that was the only name I had to give them."

This should make me happy. It's supposed to be sort of funny and sweet, right? Instead, it just makes my stomach drop and my eyes burn with tears. Everything is just so awful for her. Because of me. I look away.

"Well, I'm glad he appreciates it. You should tell him that I got Angel detention," I say, my joke thickened by the tears.

She sighs. "I'm sure that'll get a laugh. And plenty of remarks."

I shrug. "Doesn't bother me. How can a bad day here compare to a good day there?" Of course, I don't know what a good day looks like in Hell, but I can imagine that it's absolutely awful, even for those who aren't being tortured all day every day.

Like Desireé had been. I swallow the lump forming in my throat.

Her face goes pained. "Can we talk about something else?"

I nod and tell her about Heaven. The real Heaven, with roads paved with gold, just like in the stories, and endless ice cream, and buildings made for people who fly. The eternally perfect sunsets with waterfalls cascading down the mountains.

She sighs longingly.

"You'll be here soon," I assure her, although it's surely a lie. How am I supposed to turn a demon into an angel? Or convince anyone in Heaven or Hell that she's not supposed to be a demon in the first place?

She nods, but she obviously doesn't believe it. It's kind of her to at least pretend to in the first place. Even now, as a demon who literally lives in

Hell, she's nothing but kind.
She's always been kind.

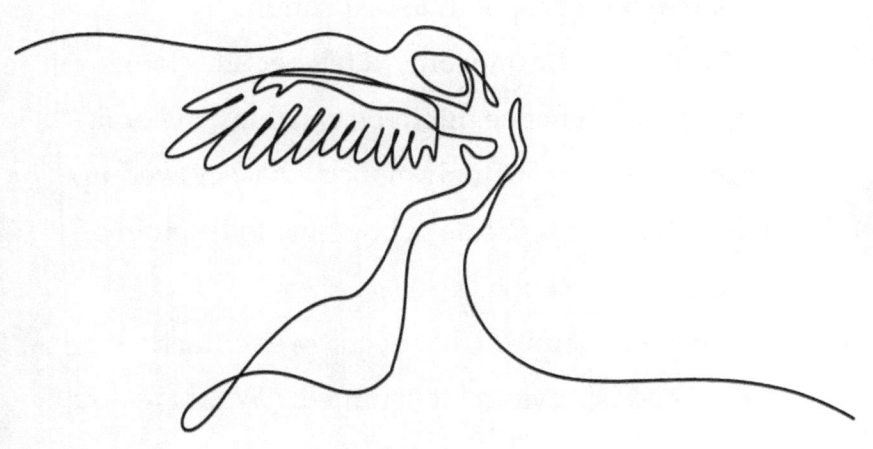

Chapter Ten

We speak nearly every night. I tell her about my day, and she avoids telling me about hers. One night, a voice hisses, "Tell her I said thanks for the non-murder."

She shoves someone away. "I already did, you ingrate," she replies, and the person laughs wickedly. That must me Marcus.

Does she have friends in Hell? Is that even a thing? I hope so. I can't imagine what it would be like to be a total outsider down there, living for an eternity of fighting and the strong possibility of a more permanent sort of death.

One night, I gasp with a realization.

"You're not the only one," I tell her after looking around like someone might be watching me or listening in. Unsurprisingly, nobody has showed up in my closet's miniscule cubby hole to listen in on a secret conversation.

She looks confused, her eyebrows scrunched together and her eyes a bit squinted. "What are you talking about?"

I continue, "Nicolai. His sister switched with him as well. Her name is Nadia. Maybe you can find her?" I try to keep the excitement out of my voice. I don't want to pressure her into doing this, but I have to at least try. For Nicolai's sake.

She frowns. "I mean, I don't know." She sighs. "There are a lot more of us here than there are of you," she says. After a pause, she repeats, "A lot."

I shrug. "I mean, I guess it's no big deal." I can't help the sinking disappointment that runs down my throat and settles in my stomach, though. If she found another wrongly-placed demon, then maybe we'd be able to do something about it. As it stands, though, there's nothing to be done. Desireé is merely one of millions. Nobody is going to hear about one person. If there's a pattern, then maybe, but it's impossible.

A tiny voice in my head points out, *The Creator might.*

I shake my head. Nobody speaks to the Creator. She's always discussed in reverent tones, like she's some big unknowable being.

I guess she is, though. I mean, she's *the Creator.* She's God. Nobody talks to God.

After I don't say anything for a while, Desireé sighs. "I can try. That's the best I can do. What does she look like?" I open my mouth, then close it again. I have no idea what Nadia looks like. And, with how different Desireé appears as a demon, it could be impossible to find her even if she's standing right in front of us next to a photograph.

"I don't know," I admit regretfully.

She sighs. "Okay. Well...I'll see what I can do." She smiles just a little. How kind of her to not point out when I'm being completely unreasonable. I smile back, but it doesn't feel right. Nothing about this situation feels right.

"I have to go," she says with a sigh. "I love you."

"I love you too," I reply, and the line disconnects. Just like yesterday, and the day before, and the one before that.

If this is all I can have with Desireé for all of eternity, it has to be enough.

When I stretch and go back out to my room, though, I watch the golden light fade as the sun sets behind the clouds, the sky pink and the waterfalls glistening.

It will never be enough.

I'm about to go to bed when a white slip of paper slides under the door to my bedroom. I go to the door and open it, looking both ways down the hall, but there's nobody there.

That's strange.

My lips tilt down on their own, and I pick up the note from the ground.

I know about the demon.

I freeze, my eyes tracing over the letters over and over again.

Someone knows.

My secret is out, and it could ruin everything.

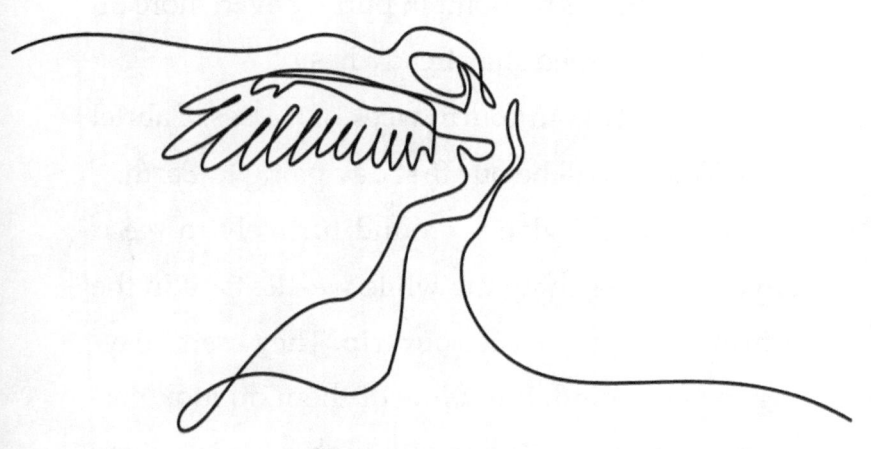

Chapter Eleven

The only thing I know for sure is that the note came from another student. If a teacher knew, I'd already be in questioning. I ask my friends at dinner on Saturday evening if they told anyone about the escape, but they all shrug and look just as confused as I feel.

I'm jumpy all day every day as the term wears on, and I can't help but look around with thinly veiled suspicion. Who sent me the note? Who are they going to tell? I try my best to go about my days as normal, but I'm far too jumpy. Desireé wouldn't be much help, so I don't tell her about the mysterious note. There's no point in putting even more on her shoulders then she already has.

At the end of our fourth week of classes, Gabriel says, "Today will be our first day going to Earth."

I tense, and I glance around furtively to see if anybody is watching me while we all stand in the infirmary to prepare for our trip. They aren't paying me any mind, but a few of them do look nervous. I take Nicolai's hand, though mine is sweaty with anxiety. No matter what, I need a friend by my side right now. It's all I can do not to throw up.

When I blink, we're still together, fingers intertwined, but we're standing in the middle of an expansive living room. Everything is far too dark, and I have to blink a few times to convince my eyes to adjust.

In Heaven, everything is so bright that it almost hurts, so both times I've returned to Earth, it seems way darker than should make sense.

Sunlight streams in through the blinds, and I avoid taking a breath. The warehouse had been rancid, and I don't want to find out if Earth just smells terrible to me now. Better to just not breathe.

"There are changes of clothing for you upstairs," Gabriel says. "You have five minutes."

All the female students crowd into a huge master bedroom, changing from our silky-smooth school uniforms into normal clothes that itch when we put them on. I have to do a couple of squats to put on the high-waisted skinny jeans that had been in the pile with my name on top.

When we meet back downstairs, Gabriel explains the procedure. "We will just be doing some basic reconnaissance. This is your first test. You all remember what it's like to be human, so just try to not look too suspicious.

I nod, and when I actually take a moment to look at Nicolai, I'm shocked to find that his hair is no longer snow white, but pale blonde. I smile. It looks adorable on him. That's when I begin to realize that everyone has a wide range of hair colors, from Daniel's long black braid to my now dark blonde hair.

"How many of you can drive?" Gabriel asks, opening a panel on the wall to reveal a series of car keys. I raise my hand timidly. The last time I drove a car, I died, but it might be nice to get behind the wheel again. It's not like I can die in a car accident a second time.

I hope.

Gabriel tosses me a set of keys, and I smile. The back of the fob has a familiar symbol on it with four overlapping circles.

This is gonna be way cooler than the ancient Camry I paid seven hundred dollars for.

When we walk out of the house, I find that we're on a farm in the middle of nowhere. The land around us is full of rolling hills and tall grass, and way off in the distance, there are horses grazing in a pasture. Where are we?

Nicolai joins me at the car I'm using, a two-seater Audi with a sporty, matte-red paint job. This is just about the coolest thing ever, and I've been to Heaven. The fleet of various sporty vehicles is in no way sensible, but I won't complain if I get to drive a sports car. I take a breath of the outdoor air, which, luckily, doesn't suffocate me like the warehouse had.

"Where exactly are we going?" Nicolai asks, but

when I start up the car, the GPS has a preloaded spot labeled as Term Two Class. "Oh," he says. "Never mind."

I put the car in gear and rip out of the driveway, laughing as the acceleration pushes me back into the leather bucket seat. Nicolai grabs the handle with wide eyes, and he stares at me.

"How did you say you died again?" he asks through gritted teeth.

I laugh once again. "Don't worry about it." I shift down as we come to a curve, then right back up through the gears. Then, a thought strikes me. "Isn't it weird that we can still understand each other on Earth? I don't speak Russian."

He shrugs, but his body remains tense. "Maybe it's an angel thing."

As I squeeze around another corner, I think of the note hidden in my cubby and the phone in my jacket pocket. I'm so glad the outfit I was given has a leather jacket, otherwise I'd have no good place to hide the device Desireé sent. It's not safe to leave it in my room anymore, not if someone knows about my secret.

"Who do you think it is?" I ask, slowing to a stop sign and slamming on the brakes. The transmission smells like burnt oil, and I frown. I can do better than this.

He chews his lip. "I don't know. It could be anyone, couldn't it? At least, any student."

I take off again, glancing in my rearview mirror to find Gabriel following me in a more sensible SUV, which has at least five other students crammed inside.

"It's not like I can bring it to one of the teachers," I say. "Desireé is supposed to be dead. Double-dead."

Eventually, the GPS takes me onto a highway. Based on the signage, we're somewhere in the United States, or perhaps Canada, but I don't recognize any of the scenery. Where I'm used to mountains and coniferous trees, there are huge sprawling fields and oak trees. It appears to be autumn.

"What year do you think it is?" Nicolai asks, and the question gives me pause.

"What do you mean?"

He looks around the car like he might find an

answer somewhere here, but he doesn't dare mess with the GPS for fear of messing up our route. At the very least, we should stay with the class. "I mean, time is different, right? So what if it's been like ten years? Or maybe it's the year before we died."

I hadn't considered that possibility. While it only feels like I've been at Theaa Academy for six months, years could've passed on Earth. Or maybe, as he'd suggested, we've gone back in time. The thought draws me through a spiral, and I have to slam on my brakes again when Nicolai shouts, "Stop light!"

My heart races, but I don't respond to his questions. What if it's before we died? What if, somewhere else, I'm still alive?

What if Desireé is still alive?

I can't help but fixate on that idea, although there's no way we're anywhere near where I used to live. I have no way to confirm her existence.

Is it even possible for us to have gone back in time? It shouldn't be. Time only goes one way.

Or does it?

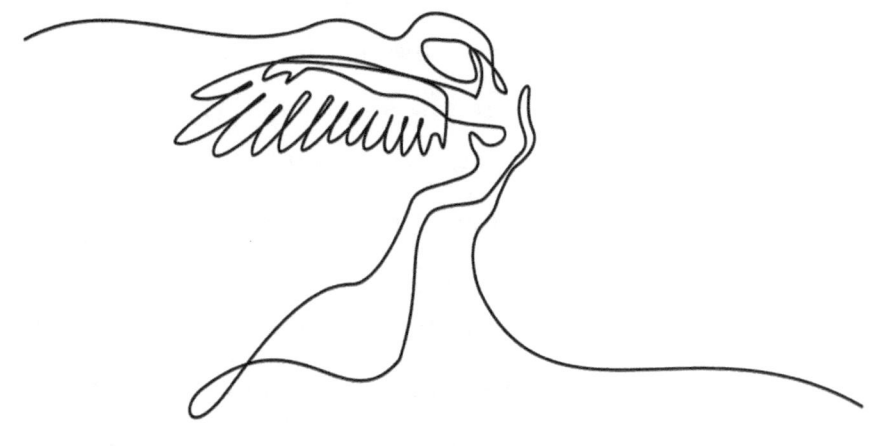

Chapter Twelve

As it turns out, it's been a year since my death. And I only know that because we pass a bank in a small town that scrolls through information on their sign. The temperature, the time, and then the date.

I sigh, letting all the tension leave my body as I take a ramp onto the interstate. There's no point in wondering about the logistics of time travel if we haven't actually done it.

Still, a nagging voice in the back of my head wonders if it's possible. Could I stop Desireé from getting in the car with me that day? Would that save her?

When sprawling suburbs give way to towering buildings, we exit the interstate.

"Are we in Kansas?" Nicolai asks, pointing out the Kansas City sign.

"No," I say. "We're in Missouri."

He frowns and mutters, "What the fuck, America?"

I smile at the perfectly reasonable question. Maybe now isn't the best time to tell him how to pronounce the state of Arkansas.

Kansas City is smaller than Portland, but only by a hundred thousand people. I remind myself that I grew up in a town of less than ten thousand, but I can't help comparing the cities instead. When I was alive, Desireé and I would take the hour drive to Portland some weekends.

The Audi's GPS leads us to a parking garage downtown. The streets are confusing and crowded, but navigable nonetheless. I only end up having to circle the block once after screwing up and missing the turn.

Nicolai makes a snide comment about it, but he

shuts up when I tell him to try and do better.

Finally, after everyone arrives, we meet near the smelly stairwell of the dimly-lit parking garage. The sky is rapidly going dark, and I can't help but shiver at the thought of being out at night in a big city. I try to remind myself that I can probably destroy anyone who tries to hurt me, or at least scare them off when I don't respond to a stab wound or a gunshot, but the darkness still makes me uneasy.

"Now," Gabriel says, "we are only checking on leads from our sources. If you find a demon, do not draw attention to yourself, and do not engage." At the last part, he stares directly at me, his eyes stormy.

It's not like I want to get into a fight with a demon. They just always seem to come after me. I don't want to try arguing with an ancient being that seems to already dislike me, though, so I just nod. It's better to not engage.

"Good, here," he says, passing out small plastic cards and newer model cell phones, although they all look a little worn. "You all need identification, as some of the places in this area only allow entrance to people who are over twenty-one."

I glance at my fake ID—I've never had one be-fore. Nicole Thomas. Nicolai shows me his. Avery Dawson. I roll my eyes. How creative. I wonder who else just had their names switched around with each other?

"You will be going off in pairs, as a whole group of you would be too suspicious. We don't want any demons getting wind of you in the area. Keep your heads low, and report to me if you see anything. The number to my phone is the only one installed in yours."

We split off a moment later, and Nicolai and I follow the GPS directions programmed into our phones. For an ancient being, Gabriel sure has fan-tastic technology working for him on Earth. I re-member trying to teach Desireé's grandma to open her email. It had taken hours, and she'd only been in her seventies, not her thousands. Or millions? It would probably be rude to ask Gabriel his exact age just for the sake of an old-people-and-technol-ogy joke.

I take Nicolai by the arm. If anyone sees us walking down the street, they'll see a normal couple. I glance at his face. Okay, they'll see an unnaturally beautiful couple, but still.

"Are you nervous?" he asks, studying my face when I look at him for a second time.

I shake my head. "Just thinking." I chew my lip, but I stop when I catch him watching me once again. "I'm fine," I insist, perhaps a little too defensively. I stare at the pavement ahead of me.

The silence between us is deafening, nearly as bad as the time he kissed me in my room and I had to rebuff his advances.

"What's that?" he asks, freezing in place and jolting me to a stop. I follow his widened eyes to an old-school diner.

"A diner?" I ask, tilting my head. Are diners suspicious all of a sudden?

He shakes his head, then drags me against the building. He nods toward the diner. "Look at the sign. Really look."

I roll my eyes but do as he says.

The longer I stare at the seemingly innocuous sign, the more it gives me a headache. Okay, that is weird. Angels don't just get headaches. Then, the shape of the logo seems to shift into something else.

The symbol for Hell in Enochian. Or, more specifically, the warped version of Enochian that demons use.

"Fuck," I mutter. When I glance into the windows, though, something there gives me pause.

More specifically, some*one*.

I can't be sure, of course. His hair is no longer an inky black, but a soft brown, and his features have filled out from their emaciated look and are no longer drained of all color.

"Marcus?" I say, my voice barely above a whisper.

The face snaps up toward me, and his eyes widen.

How the hell did he hear me?

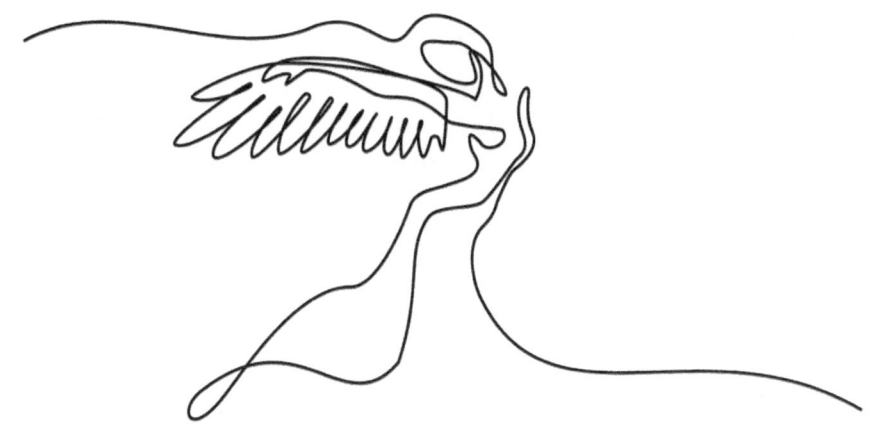

Chapter Thirteen

"We have to go," I say urgently, pulling on Nicolai's arm. Marcus is staring at me, and he says something to the person sitting across from him. Another demon, presumably. Is everyone in there a demon? I shudder. This is about as unsafe as we can be in the whole universe.

Nicolai gives me a questioning look, then turns back to the window, after a moment, his jaw drops. "Is that—"

I drag him by the arm and turn a corner into the nearest alleyway.

"Did he see us?" I ask, but I know he had. He'd

made direct eye contact with me. There's no way we've gone unnoticed.

"He did," a husky, amused voice says, and I spin around, slapping my hand over my racing heart.

Demons can teleport on Earth?

Can Angels?

"We don't want any trouble," Nicolai says, taking half a step back toward the street.

Marcus shakes his head, and his soft hair flops over his eyes. He has to brush it away to look back at us, his gaze penetrating.

"Nice to see you again, Avery Two," he says.

I open my mouth to ask what he means, but then remember that everyone in Hell thinks Avery is Desireé's name.

"Likewise," I say. Last time I saw him, I thought he was going to kill me. Now, though, he looks a lot more like a normal human boy. I've killed a demon in the past, but, at the time, I hadn't known that they were humans. With feelings and lives. And, apparently, senses of humor if I'm reading the expression on his face correctly.

Nicolai gapes at the whole interaction.

"Is there something wrong with your..." Marcus gives a pointed look at our still intertwined arms. "...Friend?" He frowns.

I drop my arm from Nicolai's and nod. Then, an idea comes to me.

"Des—Avery," I correct, "Isn't the only one that was switched." I gesture to Nicolai. "His sister took his place as well."

Marcus's eyes narrow. "And why does this matter to me?"

I'm still not totally convinced that Marcus isn't going to kill us both, but it's worth asking.

"Do you think you'd be able to find her?"

Marcus bursts into laughter, doubling over. I grit my teeth. His hysteria goes on for far too long, and my blood pressure rises.

"No need to be a dick about it," I mumble. At that, Marcus goes from being ten feet away to being right in my face. I stumble back against the wall, and he braces his arms around me, trapping me in front of him.

"I did my favor," he says, and, this close, his canines seem a bit enlarged, and his eyes are just a little off. His sulfuric breath washes over me, but I don't turn away. I will not back down. I will not show weakness. "If you want something else, how about you ask your girlfriend?"

Despite every part of my body begging me to run away, I roll my eyes. If he wanted to kill me, he would've brought reinforcements. Right? If I'm wrong about his intentions, my life is on the line. "Whatever. How about you go ahead and grab a burger. Maybe a milkshake. It'll help you chill the fuck out."

His eyes twinkle, and he surprises me by pulling away and laughing once again, although he doesn't break down like before. This is just a single short bark.

"I can see why she likes you," he says. "You're just as ruthless as she is. More, even."

After the comment, he disappears. I don't get to ask what he meant by that.

Desireé isn't ruthless. She's always been a kind, gentle soul. Even when she was a demon at Theaa Academy, she never once acted ruthless or dangerous.

I conclude that he'd been wrong. That's the only explanation. He doesn't know anything about Desireé.

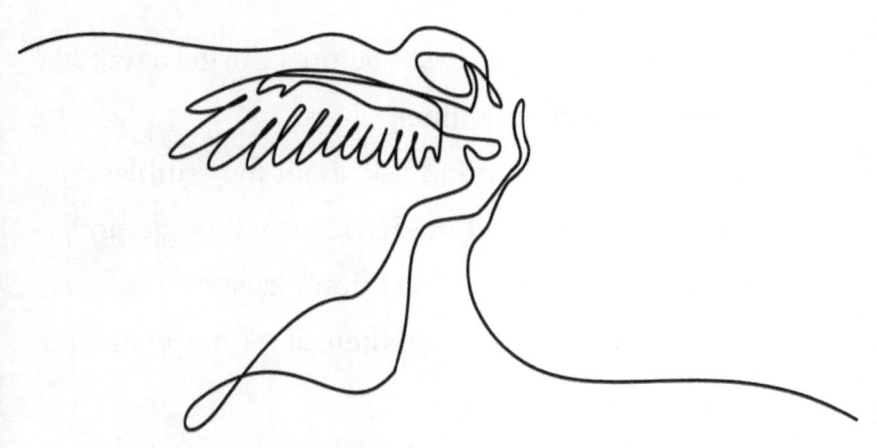

Chapter Fourteen

We don't mention Marcus's presence or the diner to Gabriel. I want to know more about Desireé's alleged ruthlessness, and if Marcus is dead, that's something I'll never find out. I knew she'd been shielding me from the torture she's endured at the hands of Hell, but I hadn't imagined that maybe, just maybe, she's done bad things, too.

When I'm back in my room that night, my phone rings. Not the flimsy human phone from my mission, which I'd returned back at the farmhouse, but the black crystal phone.

I answer it, and Desireé looks concerned as soon

as her face comes into focus.

"Are you okay?" she asks before I can get a word in. "I heard about the diner."

I sigh. "Fine." Should I ask about the "ruthless" comment Marcus had made? If I do, though, and it's a lie, then it'll seem like I don't trust her.

She frowns back at me, then darts her eyes to the side.

"What?" I ask. I am glad to be speaking with her, I really am, but today is the first time I've realized that I don't actually know her anymore. We may have been close on Earth, but for her, it's been years in Hell. How much has changed since we died? She'd seemed so broken when she'd been hiding out in my room at Theaa, but I hadn't thought to push her about her life—or, more accurately, after-life—in Hell. It hadn't seemed appropriate.

"You haven't told anyone, have you?" she asks. "About the diner, I mean."

I shake my head. "Of course not!"

A pained smile comes across her face. Why does she care about the diner? Or, more importantly, why does she know about it? "Good."

I hold back a frustrated sigh, and her eyes tighten.

I'm not being fair. I know that. Her life is a million times harder than mine. I shouldn't judge her strangeness, and I shouldn't push her secrets. But I don't really know what to think at this point. It had seemed so simple just yesterday. Desireé and I are meant to be together. But now, I'm not totally convinced I even know her anymore.

"Will you be on Earth again soon?" she asks, a spark of hope hidden in the back of her tone. That tiny bit of hope breaks me apart. I can't possibly stay upset when it's clear how important these talks are to her. They're important to me, too. I need to stop doubting her right now.

"Next Friday," I say, then pause. "I can't be totally sure when that will be on Earth, though. Because of time being so weird."

She nods, seemingly lost in thought.

I can't help but ask, "Why?"

A slow smile spreads across her face, this one actually reaching her eyes. Her fangs are revealed below her blood-red lips, and I shiver. "Because

I'm going to meet you there."

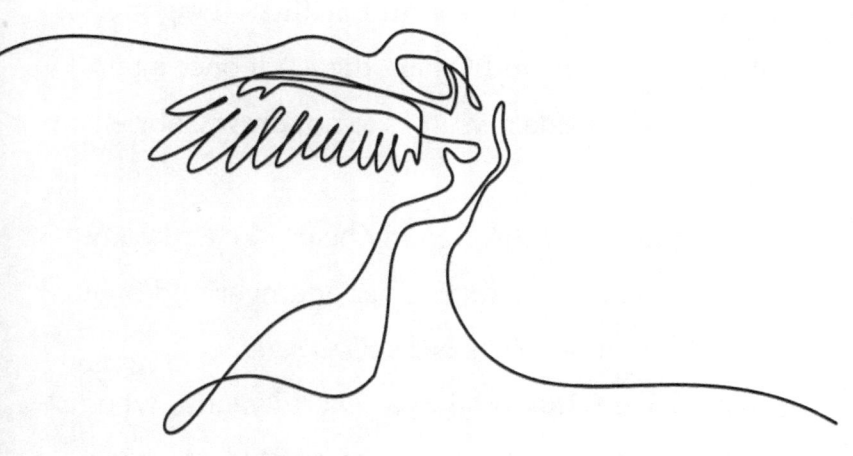

Chapter Fifteen

The week passes in a blur. The ceremony was supposed to be goodbye for Desireé and I. It had been the end. And now we talk on the phone every night, and I'm going to see her. Each day passes like a year, and I can't focus on anything that happens throughout. At one point, Huỳnh nicks me with one of her daggers in our weapons class, and Gabriel has to heal the small wound.

By the time I walk into class on Friday, I'm practically vibrating with a heavy mix of excitement and nerves. I'm going to see Desireé. In person.

We arrive in the same farmhouse as before,

tucked far out in the country with no neighbors for miles. Nicolai and I share the Audi once again, and I try to subdue myself as to not draw Gabriel's attention.

Her name runs through my heart like a melody. Desireé. Desireé. Desireé. Over and over and over again. She's here. She's here. *She's here.*

The drive to town takes an eternity, and, when we finally split up to go on our patrols, my heart lodges firmly in my throat.

Can I do this?

What if I can't handle it?

What if I'd been overlooking something in her before? What if she's just too different?

I remind myself that I spoke to her just last night, and she assured me that she'd see me in town.

My arm is looped through Nicolai's once again, and I cling to him as though my life depends on it. It very well might. I'm not sure I'd even be able to walk without his help.

"It'll be okay," he mumbles, squeezing my upper arm with his free hand reassuringly.

I grit my teeth. "Right." But I'm not so sure it

will. Has she changed even more since I last saw her?

Ruthless, Marcus had called her. I haven't seen any of that ruthlessness in her face over the phone, but her image is always weak and distant. Probably because we're communicating between Heaven and Hell, something that's not supposed to happen.

Before we make it to the diner, a hand wraps around my dangling arm and drags me into the dark alleyway. I'm so startled that I almost scream, and a hand slaps over my mouth.

Nicolai frees himself from my grip, and my eyes are taken by a pair of soft blue eyes with a gold spot in the right iris.

Before I can even take in her very human form, Desireé's lips are on mine, consuming me like I'm air and she's drowning. And that's all that matters. In the moment, I don't care how ruthless Marcus had claimed she was. I don't care that she's a demon. She's mine, and nothing in the universe will take her away from me.

When she pulls away, I half expect to see a demonic figure with too-pale skin, inky black hair, and leathery wings that block out all light, but there's none of that. There's just a redheaded girl with a soft smile and freckles like constellations across her face. She looks exactly how I remember her from Earth, all traces of the demon gone.

"I missed you," she mumbles, kissing me once again, but this time, her lips only brush against mine for an instant.

I smile. "I missed you, too."

She takes my hands in hers and kisses my knuckles.

Nicolai clears his throat. "I'll, uh, give you guys a minute. And keep watch." He backs out of the alley and goes just around the corner where we can't see him, but his presence is still obvious to me. An angel's aura is nothing like that of a human, so he can't exactly hide from me. Desireé, on the other hand, has no aura. It's like standing next to a black hole.

She pulls me further into the darkness of the alleyway, then drags me to the ground so we can lean against the wall. I don't think about how dirty this ground must be. It doesn't matter anyway, right? I'm not gonna get a disease. Eternal beings don't get tetanus from a broken beer bottle.

She sighs and leans her head against my shoulder. I brush her hair out of her face and look into her eyes, although the angle is awkward. I would stand a million years of discomfort just to see her, though.

"This is nice," she says.

I look around at the garbage and rot in the alley, then nod in agreement. "It is," I admit.

It's not ideal, but we're together. It's almost like we're alive again.

I should be asking her about her life in Hell, the venomous words that Marcus had spat at me, but I don't. I just breathe her in and hold on tight. The time is brief, but nobody can take it from us.

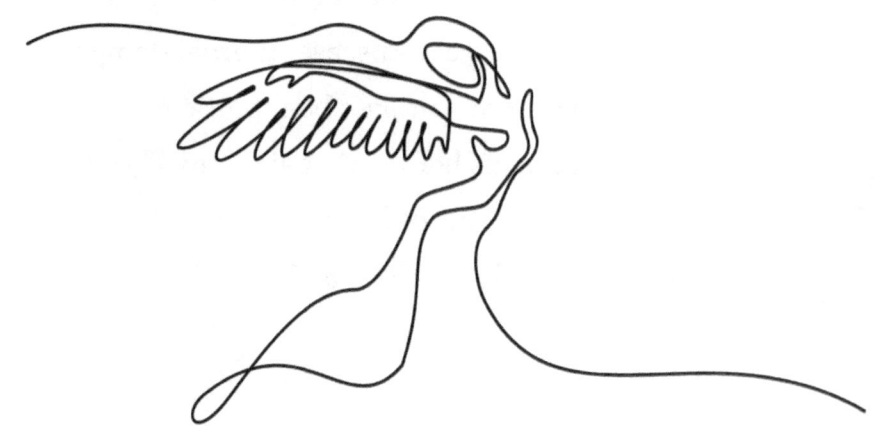

Chapter Sixteen

We don't tell anyone about the secret meetings. Even Huỳnh and Gabe don't know about them, and they're as close to me as Nicolai.

But it's not safe to tell them. It's hardly safe for Nicolai to know, but we don't have much of a choice. Our outings are brief, and we're required to have a partner. If I want to spend any time with Desireé, Nicolai has to know about it.

The meetings are short yet sweet, like samples of cake frosting stolen in the kitchen when nobody is looking. It's all we have, and it's everything.

If I could just have this for eternity, these clandestine meetings and stolen kisses, maybe it could be enough.

It should be enough.

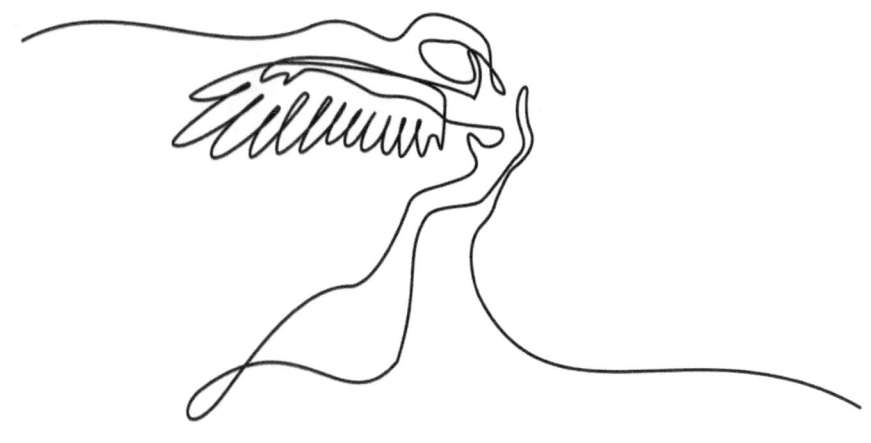

Chapter Seventeen

There's a folded piece of paper in my uniform pocket when I return to my room from one of our many outings. It couldn't be from Desireé, as I'd been wearing a pair of leggings and a tank top when I met up with her in the warm summer air. It's impossible to keep track of the date when we show up on Earth. Last week, it had been the dead of winter, the streets lines with gross mushy snow. The week before, it had been Autumn again. Who knows what it will be next time?

The note definitely hadn't been there when I left my room this morning, though. Maybe it's a class note I'd taken down and put in my pocket and promptly forgotten about. That's probably it. An assignment or something.

I unfold the thick paper carefully, expecting notes on Heavenly politics or something, but the handwriting is hasty and unfamiliar. It takes me a moment to decipher it, but when I do, my body turns to ice.

Confess your secret or you'll regret it.

There's nothing else on the paper, although I flip it a few times just to be sure. Still nothing. Who wrote this? I turn and look around as if they're in my room, lurking in one of the corners or pressed against the ceiling, but that's absurd. Still, the hairs on the back of my neck prickle.

I go to Nicolai's room, a space I rarely enter. I whisper his door number and knock urgently. I try to keep my face flat in case anybody is watching, but I can't help my fist pounding on the door with increasing desperation. As soon as the door swings open, I storm in.

"Did you write this?" I demand, shoving the note into his chest. Nicolai seems dazed, and he stares at me like I'm an alien. He's no longer in his uniform, instead sporting a t-shirt and jeans, his wings out of their harness and stretching across the space. His room is dark and cozy, lit by candles instead of bulbs, and his bed's blanket is made of a plush midnight blue material that I want to dive into. Somehow, I doubt this matches the dank apartment in Russia he's told me about.

"No," he says, tone flushed with shock, before he even glances at the paper I'd forced on him.

He scans it, his eyebrows scrunching together.

He doesn't reply, just reads the note over and over.

"Well?" I ask, unable to help my pacing. This is a crisis, and he doesn't seem to be reacting correctly. Shouldn't he be panicking? Or angry? Anything other than the slight confusion marring his features.

He frowns and looks back at me. "Where did you find this?"

"In my pocket," I say. "I think it was after the trip to Earth? But I can't be sure. Anyone could've slipped it in and I probably wouldn't have noticed." I shake my hands out in an attempt to get rid of the rising tension in my body, but it doesn't fix it. "You know, magic and all that."

He sits on his bed, his wings resting down around him like a knight's cloak.

"This is a problem," he finally says.

I bark out a laugh. "No shit."

I want him to say more, to assure me that it's gonna be alright, but he doesn't. He just keeps looking at the note and then back at me, the wrinkles in his forehead getting deeper and deeper. I half expect his skin to crack open like stone, but that's absurd.

"Are you gonna say anything?" I burst.

He looks at the ground and shakes his head. "I don't know what you want me to say."

Another laugh rips out of me. Am I becoming hysterical? I've never been hysterical before. "I want you to say it's fine. That it's a bad prank. Anything." The corners of my eyes sting.

He sighs and sets the paper on his bed.

"I think you know what this means," he says, standing and walking toward me slowly as if I might spook like a horse. He puts his hands on my shoulders, and the weight grounds me.

"No," I say, setting my jaw. "I can't."

His pale eyes pierce mine. "Avery, you have to stop seeing her. If you're found out, we have no idea what could happen to you."

I scrunch my eyes tight and shake my head, tears spilling out as my heart pounds at my ribcage. "No," I whisper. The word breaks me.

Nicolai takes me in his arms, holding me tight. I don't know what I'd do without him, honestly. He holds me while I fall apart, sobs wrenching out of my body.

"I just got her back," I cry. "It's not fair."

He rests his chin on top of my head. "I know," he says. "I know."

I sniff, pressing my forehead against his chest. "I can't let her go."

He sighs. "You have to."

I know he's right. If I keep seeing Desireé, then we'll get caught, and not just by whoever wrote this note.

If I don't stop this relationship now, who knows

what could happen to us?

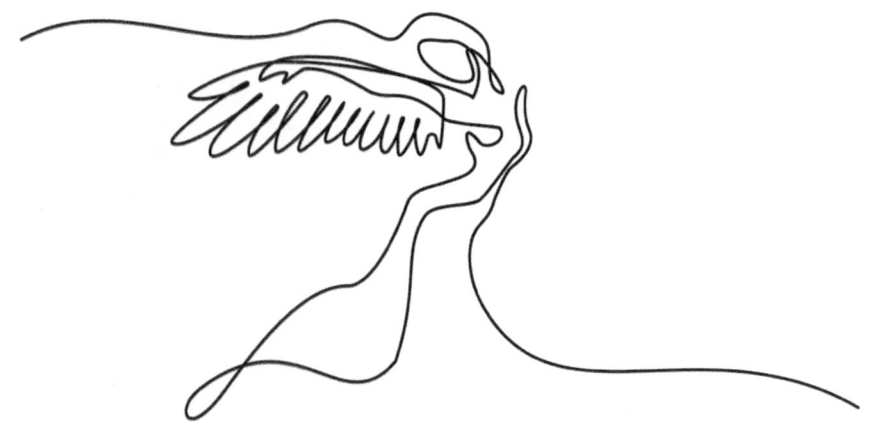

Chapter Eighteen

Everyone is a suspect now. I can't look at anybody without wondering if they wrote the note, especially other second-term students. It has to be one of them, right?

It could be Daniel, who's always nervous at the idea of demons. It could also be Jenine, the girl who hasn't spoken to me much since we had martial arts together last term. Honestly, though, it could be anyone. It's impossible to know for sure.

I don't meet up with Desireé on patrols anymore. And we don't talk as often as we used to. I'm too afraid of being caught. It's not safe for us to be in constant contact, and my heart wrenches at the thought of the Archangels finding out she's still alive.

I walk into Demon Tracking and Awareness with a slump in my step, and I don't pay nearly enough attention. I open the book to read where I'm supposed to, and I take half-assed notes, but that's all. I just can't stop wondering who's onto me, who knows about Desireé.

"Avery," Gabriel calls, and I snap out of my haze. Everyone is packing their things and leaving, and I hadn't even noticed. "I'd like you to stay for a moment so I can have a word with you."

Great. So now, on top of having to find a student that's going to out me to the Archangels, I'm in trouble in class for being distracted. I'll have to come up with a good excuse, and fast.

"I'll wait up for you," Nicolai mumbles. We're supposed to have a flying lesson this afternoon. He's very nearly to the point where he can actually stay in the air, and to celebrate, we have a trip to the city planned for this weekend.

I walk up to the front of the room, trying to seem

disinterested.

"What's up?" I ask, slinging my bag over my shoulder.

Gabriel's eyes pierce mine, and I shiver. He's always been a bit off-putting, but right now, he looks especially dangerous.

"Let's speak in my office," he says with a frown. I shrug and follow him, sitting in one of the chairs across from his desk. He sits in the leather chair behind the desk, setting his elbows on the mahogany surface and twining his fingers together.

"Is there something wrong?" I ask. I just have to be casual. The only thing he could possibly need would be for me to pay more attention in class.

He blinks slowly, then reaches in his blazer's inner breast pocket.

"Is this yours?" he asks, and the last thing I'm expecting is in his hand.

My black crystal phone.

I swallow, and my heart beats harder than ever. I just have to stay calm. Maybe he doesn't know what it is. It's not angel technology, after all.

Although I guess that's part of the problem. My

palms begin to sweat, and I keep my hands rested in my lap.

"What is it?" I ask innocently. His eyes instantly harden, and the door shuts behind me. I startle and turn, and Azrael is standing behind me, a grim expression on her face.

"There's no point in lying, Avery," she says. Her tone is filled to the brim with disappointment, and her eyes betray her broken heart. I swallow.

"I don't know what you're talking about." My voice comes out as a strained breath, though. It would be obvious to anyone that I'm lying, and these two are ancient beings who've lived through the spark of humanity.

Gabriel sighs and drops the black crystal on the desk. It clatters, and I tense like I've just heard a gunshot. "We found this in your room," he says. Then, his jaw ticks. "The first time I caught you with the demon," he spits, "I left you a warning in hopes you would confess."

My heart sinks. It hadn't been another student, but Gabriel all along. Why hadn't I considered this to be a possibility? Strategy-wise, it makes sense.

It's a lot easier for him to prove my guilt when he's been spying on me throughout the term.

He continues, "When you didn't, I left you a final note. You have been given three chances, Avery, and you've failed us at every single turn."

I gape, opening my mouth to speak, but I don't have the words. There's nothing I can say. I've been found out. The Archangels know.

Azrael's hand rests on my shoulder. "I don't want to do this," she says. Before I can ask what she means, the world goes dark.

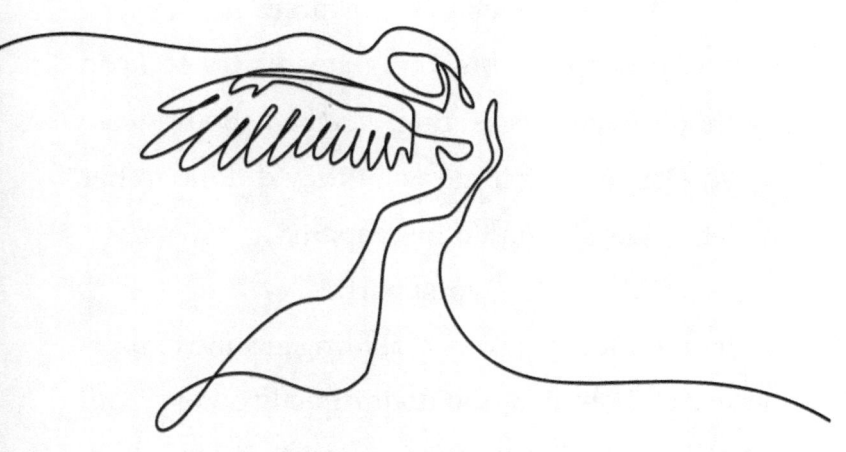

Chapter Nineteen

There's a prison in the bowels of Theaa Academy. I had no idea it existed until now, as I await my trial. The bars are made of solid titanium, and my cot is nothing more than a thick slab of marble. My wings are bound to my back by an enchanted silver chain not unlike those used to restrain demons, and they strain to break free.

Does Nicolai know what happened to me? Do Gabe and Huỳnh? I shiver at the thought of what they might be doing to me. Will I be killed again and sent to purgatory? Will I be imprisoned for eternity?

Will I be sent to Hell to be tortured?

I try to keep my breathing steady, try to keep my thoughts from spiraling. Maybe I should have forced Desireé to tell me what they'd done to her in Hell. At least then I'd be prepared.

The waiting is the worst part.

Finally, after three days of sitting around expecting my punishment, the door directly across from my cell opens. I half expect it to be Desireé, here to rescue me and take me away. Maybe we could hide out on Earth forever, hiding from the angels so that we never get punished.

Instead, though, it's Azrael. Her expression is different from the last time I saw her. Before, it had been filled with pity and sadness. Now, though, it's hard and cold.

"Avery," she says.

I walk up to the bars and wrap my fingers around them. "Azrael, please," I say. I know that begging won't get me anywhere, but I have nothing left to give. "Cain switched us. Desireé isn't supposed to be in Hell. I only did it because I knew she was innocent."

This is a half-truth at best. Even if she'd done something to deserve Hell, I don't know that I could have washed away my love for Desireé as easily as I claim. My time with her would have happened if she'd been the worst demon of all.

She might be, I remind myself. Marcus's words course through me.

She shakes her head. "It's too late for that."

I close my eyes and nod. I knew that there was a risk in seeing Desireé. After everything, though, I know for a fact I would do it all over again. As long as Desireé is safe, I won't regret my actions. I won't regret loving her.

"What's gonna happen to me?" I ask.

She frowns. "We haven't gotten to that yet."

I evaluate her face, looking for a motive and coming up short. "Then why are you here?"

It can't be anything good.

She sighs. "The demon...Desireé, has been brought into custody."

I suck in a breath. "You can't," I say, my voice going from hopeless to desperate in an instant. "Please, I'll do anything."

"She's a demon, Avery. How do you not understand this? Demons must be eliminated."

Tears openly fall down my cheeks, plummeting to the floor like rain. "Please," I gasp. "Please."

It won't help. Of course it won't.

Azrael shakes her head and walks away.

Why would she come here just to tell me that? I tug at the bars, but they don't so much as rattle. There's nothing I can do.

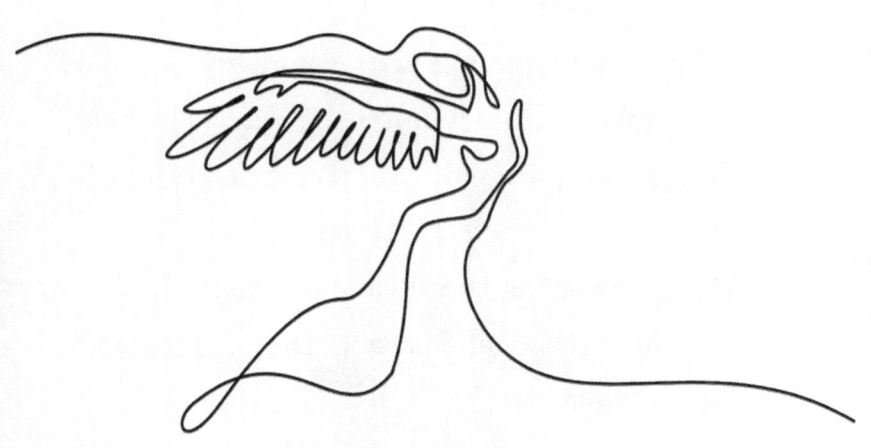

Chapter Twenty

A rustling in the night wakes me. This must be it. I take in a deep breath, then sit up and look around.

A mumbled, "Shit," draws my eyes to the floor.

"Nicolai?" I ask.

He's lying on the ground, trying his hardest to bring his wings back under control. He must have tripped over them in the cramped space.

"Shhh," he says, rushing up to the cage bars. He uses them to pull himself back to a standing position. "We only have a few minutes."

"What are you—" before I can ask, though, he

covers my mouth.

"They're going to kill you. Soon. Huỳnh is distracting them, but they're on the way." He swallows and looks around. "They've brought in Michael."

The name sends shockwaves through me. Michael. The Archangel Michael. The biggest, baddest angel there is.

"What are you gonna do?" I ask.

He looks over his shoulder, but nobody seems to be coming.

Yet.

"What I have to."

He takes my face in his hands, and, for half a second, I think he's going to kiss me again. I very nearly recoil in preparation. Instead, though, he mumbles a few words in Enochian.

"They're going to keep Desireé for the end of term ceremony," he says after he's finished his chanting. My mind begins to turn to fuzz. I have to repeat his words in my head to process them. What has he done to me?

"But what—"

He shakes his head. "There's no time. We're going to try to get her out, but if we can't…"

He doesn't continue. I blink, and his face begins to turn blurry. What's happening to me? I try to speak, but my tongue is too heavy.

He presses his lips to my forehead affectionately. "It'll be okay," he promises, his words slurred like he's speaking to me underwater.

At that moment, an impact slams into me, knocking the breath out of me like I've been hit by a truck.

The screeching of metal and rush of water overtake me, and I fade away.

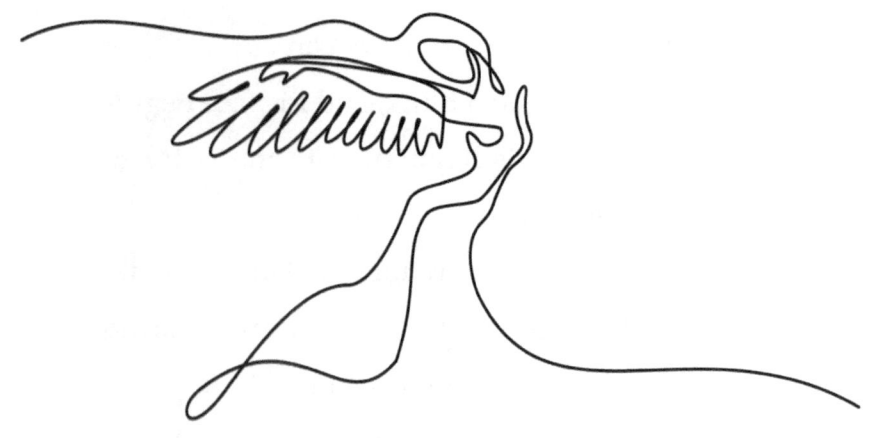

Chapter Twenty-One

When I open my eyes again, I have to blink away the light. It's nothing like the mystical brightness of Theaa Academy, though. It's an artificial fluorescence, and I lift my hand above my face to block it out. When I take a breath in, I choke on the tepid air filled with chemicals and death.

"You're awake," someone says, their relief palpable. A hand wraps around mine, and I snap my head to the side.

What the hell?

His face is somber and worn, but sober. Something I haven't seen in a long time. Years. Still, I know the face instantly. A face I thought I'd never see again.

"Dad?" I say.

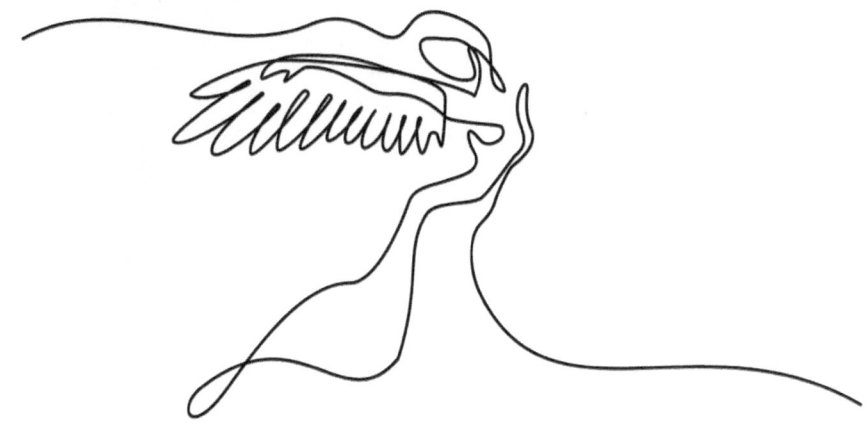

Chapter Twenty-Two

I'm on Earth.

Earth.

I'm not dead. This isn't purgatory.

Nicolai's Enochian words begin to solidify in my head, but I can't be certain of the translation. It had all happened so fast, and my brain is still a bit mushy.

"We thought we'd lost you," Dad says. His words don't make sense, and his words are filled with grief.

I shake my head. "No, I don't..." But there's nothing I can say. The words just don't come to me. One minute, I'd been in the dungeon in Theaa Academy, and the next, I was here. In a hospital room, my father by my side.

How is this even possible? I've been dead for nearly a year!

Huỳnh's words fade into my mind. *Time works differently in Heaven.*

Had Nicolai sent me back? To the moment I died? Am I alive?

Am I...human?

I sit up, expecting my head to rush. After all, I'm in a hospital. I should feel woozy. But I don't. I feel great.

I stand up, half expecting my once bad ankle to bring me crashing to the ground, and Dad reaches out like he's going to grab me, but he seems unsure of his actions. "Uh, I don't think you're supposed to move." He seems desperate and confused, though, so I rush to the restroom and stare at myself in the mirror.

My hair is back to its normal dark blonde color, but it's still got that wavy sheen that it had when I was in Heaven. I don't have any bandages on, and there isn't even an IV in my arm like I've seen in movies.

Would a needle be able to penetrate my skin? A human needle surely wouldn't be able to hurt an angel.

I turn around, and the back of the paper dress is open from the waist up. There's an upside-down V shape on my back, almost like a bruise.

My wings.

They're still there, somewhere. Somehow. But I have no idea how I'd even summon them on Earth. I whisper a spell I have memorized by now, and my sword materializes in my hand, its pearlescent handle reassuring.

It had been real. It had all been real.

And I'm still an angel.

A knock sounds at the restroom door.

"Avery, sweetie," a female voice calls gently, "I need you to open the door." I spin around and look at the weapon in my hand. I whisper another Enochian spell, and it disappears.

If Nicolai had been able to send me back in time, would he have done the same with Desireé after rescuing her? Is she somewhere nearby?

I open the door, and a tall woman with golden-brown skin and dark hazel eyes stares down at me, a gentle smile on her full lips. She's wearing a doctor's outfit, scrubs and a long white coat. She even has a stethoscope around her neck.

"See? That wasn't so bad," she says. She rests a gentle hand on my upper arm. I have to find Desireé. Now. "Let's get you back in your bed. You had quite a fall."

I shake my head. "I can't—"

But another interruption stops me. Another woman enters the room, this one wearing jeans and a t-shirt. I recognize her.

Why is Desireé's mom here? Is Desiree in a room near mine? She looks totally shell-shocked, and she rushes over and pulls me into her arms, something Dad hadn't done. The difference between my distant parent and Desireé's affectionate one is stark.

After a moment, her body begins to tremble.

"Are you okay?" I ask, pulling away. She's clearly not. Now that I have the chance to study her, her eyes are red and puffy, and her hair and clothes are distressed. "What's going on?"

She looks at the doctor, then at my dad, but she doesn't make eye contact with me.

"Sweetie, we need to talk," Dad says.

Every part of me freezes, and in that moment, I know exactly what he's going to say before he says it.

"Desireé is dead," he says.

They'd failed.

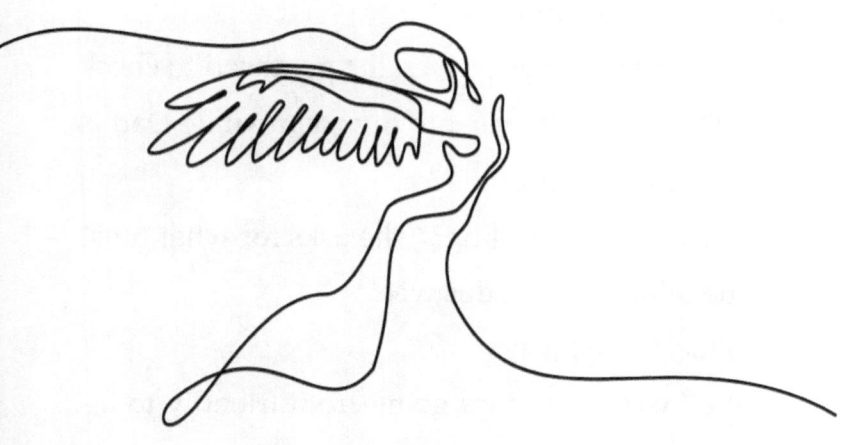

Chapter Twenty-Three

I'm trapped in the hospital for another two days, although it's unclear why. I have zero injuries, and Dr. Nassar doesn't perform any tests on me, other than asking me how I feel. Multiple times. It's frustrating and impossible. I have to get out of here, find out how to get to Desireé and save her, but I don't actually know how to teleport anywhere. That's a skill I haven't learned yet. How am I supposed to do anything productive if I can't fly or teleport? All I can do is summon my sword, but that's not helpful when I can't even find the enemy.

Dad is uncharacteristically attentive, and it frustrates me to no end.

The day I'm finally given the go-ahead to check out, Dr. Nassar comes into my room while Dad is signing paperwork.

"How are you feeling?" she asks for what must be the billionth time this week.

"Fine," I say.

She frowns, her face going from friendly to intimidating in a snap. She glances at the door. Dad is at the nurses' station, signing page after page of release forms.

"And how do you plan on rescuing Desireé from Heaven?"

It's like all the air has been sucked out of the room. I dart my eyes to the door after making brief eye contact with her, but it's closed now. What the hell is this?

"What are you talking about?" I ask, trying to play it off.

Dr. Nassar rolls her eyes and crosses her arms. "You know exactly what I'm talking about."

I wrap my arms around myself, suddenly feeling more exposed than I ever have. If this woman knows about the war, about my situation with Desireé, then how can I trust that she has my best interests at heart?

She sighs. "If I wanted to send you to purgatory," she says slowly, as though I won't be able to keep up otherwise, "I would have had plenty of chances before now."

My throat closes up, and I swallow so I can speak. "Which side are you on?"

She smirks and sits in the leather chair my dad has been spending a lot of time in. "People like you and me don't have sides."

I want to tell her that's untrue, but I'm not sure if I can. I'd been wrongly placed in Heaven, and then I'd been cast out for pointing out the unfair system. And there's no way I'd ever be accepted by Hell, not without extreme measures.

"Fine," I bite back, standing up. "I don't have a plan. I have no idea what to do, no idea where they're even keeping her."

Dr. Nassar raises an eyebrow and waits.

"Seriously! I know that demons are kept in a

warehouse somewhere on Earth. But they could be anywhere!" I ball my hands into fists. I want to scream, want to hit something. Now there's someone here who knows the situation, but I can't express myself to her properly.

Just then, the door opens, and Dad peeks back in. "You ready to go home, kiddo?" he asks. He looks horribly drawn, and I almost want to hug him for the first time in years. Almost.

I grit my teeth and nod.

"Well," the doctor says, standing. "Don't let me keep you. I just need you to come back for a checkup in one week. Otherwise, my door is always open."

Dad smiles wearily and shakes her hand. "Thanks for everything, Dr. Nassar," he says.

She smiles, the expression wicked rather than friendly, and looks at me while holding out a business card to Dad. "Please," she says, "call me Lilith."

KATE HALL is a full time traveler, dog owner, artist, wife, and reader. She believes in wild things like love, magic, and basic human decency. Some of her least favorite things include selfish people, eating fish, and tornados. *Sign up for her mailing list for exclusive access to free short stories!*

www.KateHallBooks.com

Twitter @KateHallAuthor

Instagram @KateHallAuthor

Books By Kate Hall

From the world of ST. MERLIN'S ACADEMY:
Smoke and Mist
Ignite the Mountain

ANGEL ACADEMY
Angel Academy
Clandestine Angel
Renegade Angel

GINGER HILLS
The Girl in the Lake
The Girl Who Won't Drown
The Girls Down Below

VAMPIRE HUNTER CHRONICLES
Night Academy
Deadly Academy
Final Academy

SOUTHERN WITCHES
Southern Charms
Southern Spells
Southern Neromancy